Yoga in School

with Neela & Friends

A story of a group of children that learn yoga in school.

Written and Illustrated by

Shayann M. Hoffer

This book is dedicated to my family

योगश्चित्तवृत्तिनिरोधः ॥२॥

yogaś-citta-vṛtti-nirodhaḥ ||2||

Yoga is the control of the mind thoughts

Patanjali's Yoga Sutra 1.2

One morning in a small town, Neela wakes up to get ready for school. She grabs her bag, meets her brother, Aiden and their cousin, London to ride the bus.

The bus ride is quiet, which gives them time to
mentally prepare for the day.

From another home two brothers,
Grant and Emmet, start walking to school.

They arrive at School Alma,
where the seeds grow with the sun and are watered by the rain.

Neela, London, and Grant go to their first class, Sound Language.
This is one of their favorite classes. Mrs. Otto starts talking,
"Good morning, today we'll be working with vowel sounds.

"Listen to your breath, slow your inhale and slow your exhale."
She raises her hands and says "Everyone, A...E...I...O...U...Excellent!
Again, now notice how your mouth changes. A...E...I...O...U...
This increases your positive energetic vibration."

Next class Aiden joins the group to learn about the country of Africa. "One special animal we find in Africa is the lion."

Lion Pose
Simhasana

Now, let's sit by bending at your knees with your feet under your hips.
Straighten your arms and hands towards your knees, spread your fingers.
Stick out your tongue, open your eyes wide,
and roar like a lion. Inhale. ROARRRRR!

The influence of the lion is illustrated in ancient stones and structures like that of the Great Sphinx. Half man, half lion, symbolizes soul protection of the Kings and Pharaohs of the time.

Sphinx Pose
Salamba Bhujangasana

Come to your belly, lift your chest,
place your arms parallel and elbows under your shoulders.

The Great Pyramids of Giza are said to have been built in relationship to the stars and constellations in the sky.

Pyramid Pose
Parsvottanasana

Like the strength of a pyramid, come to your feet and step
your left foot back, creating a triangle with your straight legs.
Bring hands together behind your back, inhale,
bring your chest toward your right knee, exhale. Other side.

In our next topic, mathematics and geometry, we find the triangle. Three or four equal triangles create a 3-Dimensional pyramid.

Triangle Pose
Trikonasana

From standing, step your left foot back, keep your right foot straight.
Both legs stay straight and arms out to the side, like the letter T.
Inhale, bring your right hand down toward your right shin.
Keep your left shoulder lifted above your right shoulder,
lift your left hand toward the sky. Other side.

By joining two triangles we find the
relationship to that of the arc,
which is a common design of a bridge.

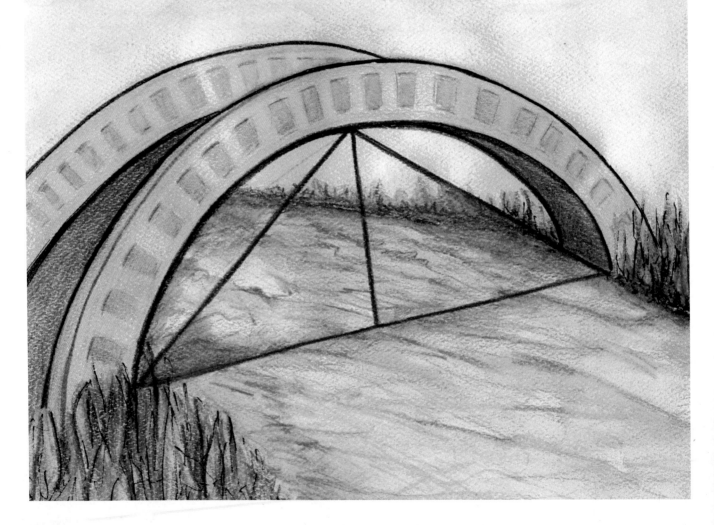

Bridge Pose
Setu Banda
Sarvangasana

From your back, bring the soles of your feet to the floor
under your hips. Bring your hands together
under your back along the floor and lift your hips.

By joining two arcs we find one of the most common shapes, the circle with 360 degrees.

From the circle we have created the wheel as one of the most useful objects to this day.

Wheel Pose
Urdhva Dhanurasana

On your back, bring your hands on the sides of your ears
and elbows to the sky. Bring your knees bent and feet on the floor
near your hips. Press your hands and feet into the floor,
slowly straighten your arms and legs, lift your hips and chest up

In the area of science and biology we find fish.
Fish have gills so they can breathe underwater.

Fish Pose
Matsyasana

From your back bring your chest up, elbows under and
toward each other, fingers up like a fin.
Bring the top of your head slowly back toward the floor,
with your chin towards the sky.
Legs can be straight like a long fish tail or
bent and crossed for a short fish tail.

Frogs are another water creature, they also live on land.
This is a form of evolution from a swimming tadpole to frog legs.
Frogs have amazing abilities using their feet, eyes, tongue, and
throat making interesting sounds like 'Ribit, Ribit, Ribit'!

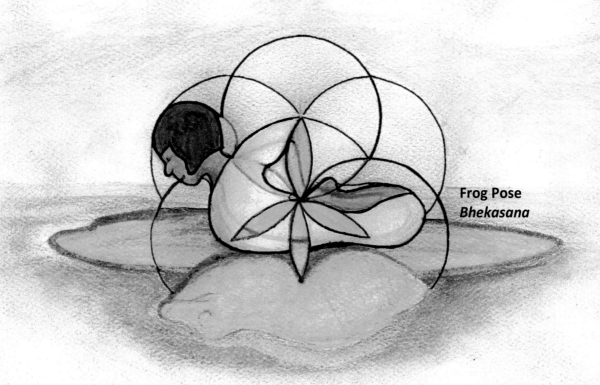

Frog Pose
Bhekasana

From your belly, bend at your knees and elbows.
Right hand to right foot and left hand to left foot.
Elbows together towards the sky and chin lifted.

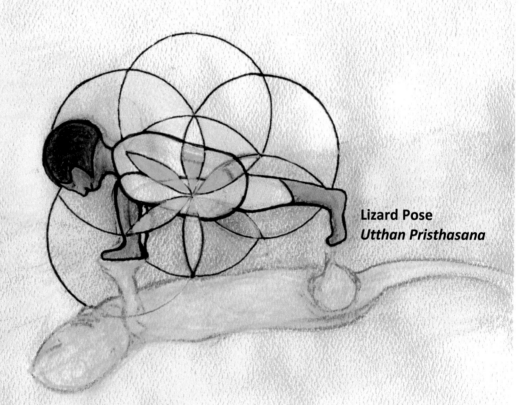

Lizard Pose
Utthan Pristhasana

From standing, bring your left foot back,
bend your right knee to locate over your right ankle.
Bring your hands to the floor around your knee,
tuck your left toes and straighten your back leg. Other side.

It's now time for 'Outside Learning' sessions, lunch, and recess.
On their nature walk London points out a crow in the tree.
Crows are one of the most intelligent birds.

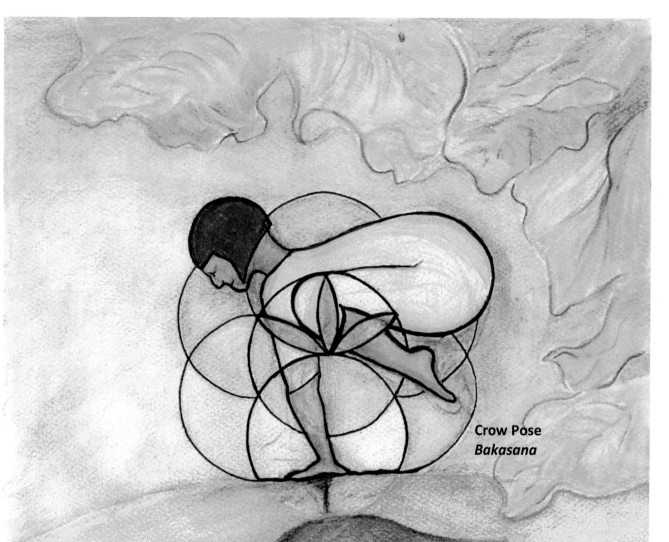

Crow Pose
Bakasana

Bring your hands to the floor, shoulder width distance.
Come to tip toes, bend your knees and bring them to your arms.
Find your arm and knee connection, come forward to lift off from
your toes to balance on your arms. Eyes up.

The class walks around the school house and notices a
boat on the pond. "Great!" Mrs. Otto exclaims,
"Now we can start talking about boats!"

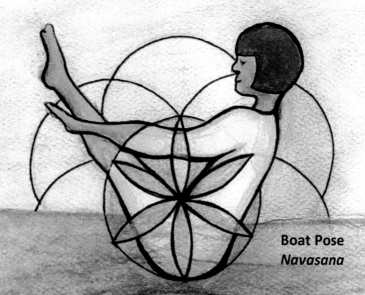

Boat Pose
Navasana

From a sitting position,
bring your knees together, balance with your hands,
keep a straight back, and straighten your legs.
Bring hands out to the sides like oars.

Mrs. Otto excuses the students. Aiden and Grant are in charge of harvesting the garden and after lunch, the compost.

They bring baskets out to the garden and start at the pea patch.

Grant suggests they try one to make sure they are ready.

They each pick one and reveal smiles in between chewing bites.

They collect pea pods, carrots, lettuce, kale, and strawberries for dessert. They bring back the food, excited to have lunch.

When they return, they see Neela and London with Emmet,
putting together the rest of the food.
They work together preparing the food and then the lunch bell rings.
The rest of the students come together into the circle.

It's Emmet's day to give thanks, he looks around the circle,
smiles and says, "I love strawberries and thanks for the kale!"
The children smile with an inside giggle,
Emmet rings the chime and lunch begins.

At the end of lunch, Aiden and Grant bring the food scraps
to the compost bin and dump the leftovers.

Tomorrow will be the day to turn the compost and add grass clippings.

Today is "Bee" day. Mr. David is waiting near the bee box with his netting on. The children stay back as he pulls out the honeycomb. He peels the comb from the screen as the bees swarm around.

Mrs. Otto and the class divide the comb and can't help
but smile from ear to ear from the sweet taste of honey.

"Now class, let's find our seat like Padma and listen." Mrs. Otto says.
The class moves into the circle and into their seat,
they cross their legs and close their eyes. She adds,
"Listen to your breath and calm your thoughts."

Lotus Pose
Padmasana

The stillness clears the area for a moment and then
all of a sudden it moves into a light humming sound,
"Hummmmmmmm…"
"Excellent everyone, thank you for listening and sharing. Namaste."

ABOUT THE AUTHOR

**Shayann M. Hoffer is a registered yoga and art teacher
that currently lives in the Pacific Northwest.**

Find her other book, ***Neela Meets Lotus*** on Amazon and Youtube

**www.neelameetslotus.weebly.com
www.shayann.massageplanet.com**

Made in the USA
Monee, IL
04 August 2022

10745096R10026